# first snow

*by* leonid gore

ginee seo books    atheneum books for young readers    new york ∗ london ∗ toronto ∗ sydney

It was time for bed. Mommy was reading a story, but Danny wasn't listening. Something was flying outside the window. "Oh, look at the snow!" Mommy said. "What is *snow*?" asked Danny. But he was too tired to hear what Mommy said.

He fell asleep.

The snow did not sleep. It flew and swirled

and danced all night long.

The next morning Mommy dressed Danny in his
warmest scarf.
"This is your first snow," she said.
"But what is snow, Mommy?" Danny asked again.
"You'll see." Mommy laughed.

Danny ran outside.

What a surprise!

All the trees, bushes, and grass were gone.

And who were these new friends?

"Hello,"
said Danny.
"Do you
want
to play?"

"I will show you a good game," said Danny.
"It's called leapfrog."

He hopped
over a little chick.

Then he leaped over a downy lamb

and bounded
over a prickly
hedgehog.

He even
managed
to jump over
an ostrich.

But the donkey
was too tall to play.
Danny tripped over
her ear and fell.

When he picked himself up,
she was gone.

"Where are you,
my friend?
Please come back!"

# Wolves!
No wonder she had run away.

Danny shivered. Suddenly it was very cold.
Then he remembered what Mommy had told him.
"When you get scared, run!" she'd said.

So Danny ran . . .

as fast as he could.

He ran in circles. He could see the wolves spreading their paws to catch him.

He ran in zigzags,
jumping from side to side.

He could feel
the wolves
spreading
their paws
to scratch
him.

Danny ran and ran,
and didn't stop until he
knew he was safe.

The wolves were gone. His friends were gone
too—all but the sleepy elephant. The elephant was
too big to be afraid of wolves.

But she was also too big to play leapfrog.
Maybe they could play something else.
"May I slide down your trunk?" asked Danny.

Wheeee!
The elephant did
not mind at all.

All too soon Danny heard Mommy calling him to come inside.

"Now do you know
what snow is, Danny?"
asked Mommy.

"Yes, Mommy. I know what snow is today . . .

. . . but I can't wait to see what it will be tomorrow!"

*To my daughter, Emily,*
*who was born on a very snowy day*

Atheneum Books for Young Readers * An imprint of Simon & Schuster Children's Publishing Division * 1230 Avenue of the Americas, New York, New York 10020 * Copyright © 2007 by Leonid Gore * All rights reserved, including the right of reproduction in whole or in part in any form. * Book design by Ann Bobco * The text for this book is set in Bernhard Modern. * The illustrations for this book are rendered in acrylic and pastels on paper. * Manufactured in China * First Edition * 10 9 8 7 6 5 4 3 2 1 * Library of Congress Cataloging-in-Publication Data * Gore, Leonid. * Danny's first snow / Leonid Gore. — 1st ed. * p.   cm. * "Ginee Seo Books." * Summary: When he ventures outside to experience his first snowfall, a young rabbit discovers that his world has greatly changed. * ISBN-13: 978-1-4169-1330-6 * ISBN-10: 1-4169-1330-0 * [1. Snow—Fiction. 2. Imagination—Fiction. 3. Rabbits—Fiction.] * I. Title. * PZ7.G659993Dan 2007 * [E]—dc22   2005013089